SKY WA

DISCARDED

Bruce County Public Library
1243 Mackenzie Rd.
Port Elgin ON N0H 2C6

VICKI C. HAYES

SADDLEBACK
EDUCATIONAL PUBLISHING

red rhino
b **OO** k s ™

With more titles on the way ...

SADDLEBACK
EDUCATIONAL PUBLISHING
www.sdlback.com

Copyright ©2014 by Saddleback Educational Publishing
All rights reserved. No part of this book may be reproduced in any form or by any means, electronic or mechanical, including photocopying, recording, scanning, or by any information storage and retrieval system, without the written permission of the publisher. SADDLEBACK EDUCATIONAL PUBLISHING and any associated logos are trademarks and/or registered trademarks of Saddleback Educational Publishing.

ISBN-13: 978-1-62250-898-3
ISBN-10: 1-62250-898-X
eBook: 978-1-63078-030-2

Printed in Guangzhou, China
NOR/0714/CA21401177

18 17 16 15 14   1 2 3 4 5

DEZ

Age: 12 … and a half

Family: has four younger sisters

Favorite Color: gold

Future Goal: to clean up the ground beneath the trees

Best Quality: bravery

Age: 13—held back a year

Most Proud of: his hair

Wants to Become: more confident

Future Goal: become an actor and star in action movies with Kath

Best Quality: being a good friend

1
DEZ

Dez flew to school. He hopped on his sky bike. He used to zoom to school. He zoomed on the sky bike path. The path went to school. The sky path was up high. It was up in the air. The houses were up in the air too. They had to be.

HOUSES

GARBAGE

The ground was covered with trash. The ground was covered with muck. It was not safe there. People lived up in the air. And kids flew to school. They flew on the sky path.

But this year Dez did not zoom. This year Dez flew slowly. He watched all the other kids. The sky path was filled with kids. Each kid had a sky bike. The bikes came in all colors. The bikes came in all sizes. Some bikes had gold stars. Dez's bike had gold stars. Dez was a Sky Watcher. Sky Watchers watched kids fly to school.

DEZ'S SKY BIKE

Only sixth grade kids could be Sky Watchers. Dez really wanted to be a Sky Watcher. This year he was in sixth grade. This year his dream came true. He was picked! He was a Sky Watcher! Dez patted his bike. He touched the gold stars. He grinned.

"Dez!" someone called. It was Jax. He was Dez's best friend. Jax flew up next to Dez.

"Have you seen any spinners?" Jax asked. Jax was a Sky Watcher too. The two boys liked to watch together.

"No," said Dez. "Not yet." He looked at the trees below him. He watched the leaves.

The trees were below the sky path. The trees were tall. They covered the ground. The trees were made of plastic. They covered all the trash and muck. The trees stopped the bad air. The trees kept the kids safe. But the trees had one bad thing. The trees had spinners.

Spinners looked like round plates. They flew up from the trees. Spinners took bike packs from kids. All the kids had bike packs. They put their books in the packs. They put their lunches in the packs. The bike packs clipped on the bikes. But a spinner could break the clips. A spinner could grab the pack. It would take the pack down. It would take the pack into the trees. Gang kids waited in the trees. They waited for the packs. Then they kept them.

"GANG KIDS"

Sky Watchers kept the packs safe. Sky Watchers stopped the spinners. Dez and Jax had to stop the spinners.

All of a sudden Dez saw something. He saw leaves shaking. The leaves were shaking on a tree below him.

"Jax!" he called. "I think I see a spinner!"

2
SPINNERS

Dez made his bike fly fast. He zoomed. A
spinner came out of the trees. It shot up. It
made a loud buzzing noise. It flew toward a
girl. The girl was on a red sky bike. She did
not see the spinner. But Dez did. Dez had to
shoot the spinner. He had to shoot it fast. It
might get the girl's pack. The spinner would
break the clips. It would make the pack fall.
It would take the pack into the trees.

Dez pulled out his spinner stunner. He flipped it on with his thumb. Spinner stunners stopped spinners with a beam of light. A special light. Dez had to shoot the spinner. He had to shoot it right in the middle. Then the spinner would lose power.

Dez watched the spinner. It was getting close to the girl. Dez had just a few seconds. He went faster on his bike. He held his spinner stunner out in front. He kept his arm very still. Then he shot his stunner.

The spinner froze in midair! Then it began to fall. It had no power. It was falling into the trees. Dez knew it would fall down. It would fall to the ground. It would fall into the muck. It would not come back.

MUCK

"Nice job!" called Jax. "You shot it just in time." He flew up beside Dez. Jax gave him a high five.

Dez grinned. He made his bike go slow. He had seven spinner shots this week! He was doing well.

"Can I win the contest?" he asked. "Seven shots are a lot."

The Sky Watchers had a contest. The contest was each week. The kids counted their spinner shots. The kid with the most shots was the winner. The winner got free time at the game center.

Dez had never won. He really wanted to.

"I don't know," said Jax. "You might win. But I think Kath has seven shots too."

"Kath wins a lot," said Dez. "She is a very good shot. It is hard to beat her."

"Yeah," said Jax. "But you will get more shots. There are more spinners this year. Mr. Munn says so. He says the older kids are in a big gang. The gang is working on the spinners. They are making more spinners. They are making the spinners go faster."

"That's bad," said Dez. "There are too many spinners now. And they go very fast.

Sometimes we can't shoot them all."

"Why do the gang kids make spinners?" asked Jax. "Why do they grab bike packs?"

"My mom told me," said Dez. "She says they need the bike packs. She says they eat the food. Then they sell the other stuff. She says it's sad. But they need the money. This is the way they get it."

"Well, I think ..." Jax stopped talking. A new noise had started.

Beep! *Beep*! It was a horn. It was a horn on a sky bike. It was beeping. A spinner was after someone!

WATCH OUT!
SPINNERS!

3
MORE SPINNERS

Dez spun around. He saw a sky bike. It was floating on the sky path. The light on the bike was flashing. The rider was a little boy. The boy saw Dez. The boy waved his arms. The boy pointed down. Dez looked down. He saw a spinner. It was flying for the trees. The spinner had a yellow bike pack.

"I'll get it," Dez called. He made his bike go fast. He zoomed down to the trees. But Dez was too late. The spinner slipped below the leaves. Dez floated in the air. He didn't want to go down. There was muck and trash under the trees. But catching spinners was Dez's job. He had to chase the spinner. Dez flew his bike slowly into the trees.

It was very dark under the leaves. Dez could not see. He made his bike float. The smell was bad.

He didn't want to stay in the trees. Maybe he should go. Maybe it was too late. Maybe the gang kids had the boy's pack.

Then Dez saw a flash of yellow. It was the bike pack. It was in front of him. It was stuck in a tree. The spinner was pulling the pack. But the pack was stuck.

BIGTIME STUCK

Dez looked for gang kids. He did not see any. But he had to watch for them. He wanted to shoot the spinner. Shoot it with light. He wanted to get a good shot. He didn't want the gang kids to stop him.

Dez had to shoot the spinner in the middle. Then it would lose power. That would be good. The spinner would drop. It would fall into the muck. But it could also be bad. The bike pack could fall. Dez wanted the pack to stay stuck. He wanted it to stay in the tree. He didn't want it to fall.

What could Dez do? Then Dez had an idea. He would fly under the spinner. Then he would shoot it. The spinner would lose power. The spinner would fall into the muck. The pack might fall too. But Dez could catch it. He knew he could.

Dez flew right under the spinner. He pulled out his spinner stunner. He flipped it on. He looked up. He pointed his stunner. He held his arm very still. Then he shot his stunner.

STEADY, DEZ...

The spinner froze! Then it fell. It fell right past Dez. It went all the way down. It went into the muck. Dez did not see it hit the muck. Dez was looking at the pack. The bike pack was still in the tree. It was still stuck. Dez flew up to it. He lifted it out of the tree. He was glad. The bike pack had not fallen. It had not fallen into the muck. Dez could give the pack to the boy.

Dez flew up. He flew out of the trees. Jax and the little boy were waiting.

"There he is!" shouted Jax.

"He has my pack!" yelled the boy.

"Now I've shot eight spinners!" shouted Dez. "I bet I win the contest."

4
INTO THE TREES

Dez and Jax helped the boy. They put the pack back on his bike. Then Jax looked around.

ALL CLEAR!
LET'S GO TO SCHOOL

"It's time for school to start," he said. "Those are the last kids." He pointed at three kids. They were last on the sky path.

"Then let's go to school," said Dez. He

was grinning. "I want to see Kath. I want to talk to her. I will tell her I got eight spinner shots. What will she say then?"

"She will say she has eight," said Jax. "She is pretty good, you know." Jax grinned.

"Then I will get nine shots," said Dez. He looked for more spinners. But the spinners had stopped. There were no more spinners. There were no more kids. It was time for school. Dez stopped grinning.

Beep! *Beep*! A sky bike was beeping!

"What is beeping?" asked Jax. "All the kids are gone."

"No," said Dez. "Look!" He was pointing way back. There was a green sky bike. The light on the bike was flashing. The boys turned their bikes around. They flew back on the path.

"Where's the spinner?" asked Dez. He looked under the green bike. He looked for a spinner. He looked for a falling pack. But there was nothing.

Dez and Jax came up to the green sky bike. A little girl was on the bike. She was crying.

"Where's your bike pack?" asked Dez. "Did a spinner come?"

The little girl pointed down at the trees.

"My bike pack is gone," she said. "I tried to catch it. But the spinner went too fast."

"I'm sorry," said Dez. "Sometimes the spinners win."

"We will fly with you to school," said Jax. "You can get a new bike pack."

"No," said the girl. "I must get my pack back." She began to cry again.

Jax and Dez looked at each other. Dez shook his head.

"It is too late," said Jax. "The spinner is in the trees. The gang kids will have your pack now."

LOOK DOWN

THE PACK IS
IN THERE

"No," said the little girl again. "You must get it. I have to have my bike pack. It has something good in it. It cannot stay with the gang kids."

Dez and Jax looked at each other again.

"Okay," said Dez. "We will try. You must go to school. Tell Mr. Munn about your pack. Jax and I will go into the trees. We will try to find your pack."

The little girl smiled. She rubbed her eyes. She began to fly down the sky path. Dez and Jax watched her go. Then they looked at each other again.

"We should not do this," said Jax.

"We said we would," said Dez. "So let's go."

5
UNDER THE TREES

Dez and Jax flew their sky bikes. They flew down to the trees. They went under the top leaves. They went into the dark below.

The smell was bad. The earth was yucky.

UP CLOSE   FAR AWAY   REALLY FAR AWAY

There were piles of trash and muck. There were swamps of dirty water. There was stinky oil. There was smelly smog. It was not good to be down here. People lived above the trees. The air was clean above the trees. The trees kept the air clean. All the houses were up in the clean air. Some workers had to go down into the trees. But no one else went down. The ground was a sad place.

Now Dez and Jax were in the trees. It was dark. They had lights on their sky bikes. They turned the lights on. The lights helped them see a little bit.

BIKE LIGHT

They could see the tall tree trunks. They could see piles of trash down below them. But they could not see much else. They

could not see a spinner. They could not see a bike pack.

"Let's fly slowly," said Jax. "I can't see very well. I don't want to hit a tree trunk."

"The lights on our sky bikes only help a little," said Dez. "We will go slowly."

The boys flew their bikes between the thick trunks. It was very quiet under the trees.

"We should float," said Dez. "We will hear a spinner if we are quiet." Dez knew that spinners made noises. Spinners made buzzing noises when they flew.

Dez and Jax made their bikes float. The

boys were quiet. They looked all around. They looked into the darkness. They waited for a noise.

"Nothing," said Jax. "I hear nothing. This is not good. We should go back up."

IN THE SKY, WHERE WE ARE SAFE

"Wait some more," said Dez. He flew his bike very slowly. He flew between the trees. Then he stopped. "Do you hear something now?" he asked.

Jax did not move. He sat very still. He could hear a soft noise. It was coming from far away. It was a buzzing noise.

"I hear it!" said Jax. "I hear a spinner.

I think it's over there." Jax pointed. He started to fly his bike to the buzzing.

"Yes," said Dez. "That must be it. Let's see if we can catch it."

Dez flew after Jax. The boys flew to the buzzing sound. It was far away. They hoped they could find it. But could they find it before the gang kids? It was very dark under the trees. They could not go fast.

Then Dez went a little bit faster. He flew up next to Jax. Then he flew past Jax. Dez was fast on a sky bike. He liked to race at school. He liked to win sky bike races. Maybe he could win this race too.

6
GANG KID

The buzzing sound grew louder. The boys were getting closer.

"There!" cried Dez. "I see the spinner!"

It was still dark under the trees. But the boys could see blue sparks. Spinners made blue sparks. The blue sparks flashed in the dark.

WISH WE HAD A FLASHLIGHT

"Where is it going?" asked Jax.

"It's going to a gang kid," said Dez. "We have to stop it."

Then there was a new noise. It was a sky bike. The sky bike zoomed past them. It was a gang kid. He was racing for the spinner. He wanted the bike pack.

GANG KID CONTROLLING THE SPINNER

"Stop!" yelled Dez. "You can't have that pack." He zoomed his bike faster. It was dark under the trees. But Dez had to win this race. He did not want the gang kid to win. The gang kid would keep the pack.

Dez went faster and faster. Soon Dez flew next to the gang kid. Then Dez moved in front. He turned his bike fast. The gang kid had to turn. But the gang kid bumped a tree. His bike lost power. The gang kid had to float. Dez and Jax zoomed away. They zoomed after the spinner.

"I can shoot the spinner," yelled Jax. He pulled out his spinner stunner.

"No!" yelled Dez. "The spinner will lose power. It will drop the bike pack. The pack will fall into the muck. We have to save the pack."

"Then what can we do?" asked Jax. "The spinner is not going to stop."

Dez had to think. What could he do? Then he had an idea. It was the idea he had before.

A BRIGHT IDEA

...AGAIN

"I know," said Dez. "Listen to this. I will fly under the spinner. I will shoot the spinner. The spinner will lose power. It will drop the pack. I will grab the pack."

THE PLAN
(IN DETAIL)

"The spinner is too fast," said Jax. "You can't do two things. You can't shoot and grab. It is too hard."

Dez had to think. Jax was right. Last time the bike pack was still. It was stuck in a tree. This time the bike pack was flying. It was stuck on a spinner. Dez couldn't do two things. He couldn't shoot and grab. What could he do? He needed a new idea. Then he knew.

"I know," said Dez. "We will work together. You will shoot the spinner. I will grab the pack. It will be hard. But I think we can do it."

Jax shook his head. "I think it will be too hard," he said.

"It will be hard," said Dez. "But we have to try."

7
THE SHOT

Jax and Dez followed the spinner. They flew fast. But they had to watch the trees. They didn't want to bump a tree. Their bikes would lose power. Just like the gang kid's bike.

LAST SUMMER WHEN I BUMPED A LOT OF TREES

The spinner flew fast. It didn't bump a tree. That would make it lose power too.

Then it would fall into the muck.

The spinner flew around the trees. The boys flew around the trees. Then Dez flew to a new place. He flew under the spinner. It was hard to fly and watch the spinner. But he did it.

Jax flew closer to the spinner. He was flying fast. He was getting to be a good racer. Jax pulled out his spinner stunner.

"This is going to be hard," Jax said to himself.

"Are you ready?" yelled Dez. He wanted Jax to make a good shot.

"I think I will miss," yelled Jax. Jax did not think he was a good shot.

"You will not miss," yelled Dez. "You will hit the spinner. Hold your arm very still."

"That's hard," yelled Jax. "I am flying too fast."

Dez had to wait. Jax needed time to get ready. The boys kept flying. The spinner kept flying. Then Jax was ready.

"Okay," yelled Jax. "I think I can do it."

"Good," yelled Dez. "Tell me when you shoot."

Jax held up his spinner stunner. He flipped it on with his thumb. He had to shoot the spinner right in the middle. He held his spinner stunner out in front of him. He kept his arm very still. He was ready.

"Now!" yelled Jax. Jax shot his stunner. Dez watched.

The spinner froze in midair! Jax had made a good shot. The spinner began to fall. It was falling into the muck on the ground. The pack began to fall too. Dez had to grab the pack. Could he do it?

Dez held out his hands. The spinner fell past Dez. But the spinner bumped him. It bumped his arm.

Could Dez grab the pack now?

8
WHAT IS IT?

Dez grabbed it! He grabbed the pack.

"Yes!" yelled Jax. "You got it!" Dez and Jax grinned at each other.

Then the boys left the trees. They left the bad smell. They flew up into the clean air. They were glad to leave.

WE DID IT!

Dez held the pack in one arm. He was happy to have the pack. But something was odd. Something in the pack was moving. What could be moving?

"Jax! Wait!" said Dez.

Jax flew next to Dez. They floated on the sky path side by side.

"What is it?" asked Jax. "Why are we waiting?"

"There is something funny," said Dez. "There is something funny in this pack."

IT'S MOVING!

Dez put the pack in his lap. Dez opened the pack. He bent over to look. Jax bent over to look.

Inside the pack was something alive.

"What is that?" asked Jax. "Is that an animal?"

It was an animal. The animal was brown. It had four legs. It had brown fur. It had long floppy ears. It had big brown eyes. It had a fluffy tail.

"I know what it is," said Dez. "I saw it in a book. It is a dog."

"A dog?" asked Jax. "What is it for?"

Dez had to think about the book. He had to think about what he read.

"Dogs used to live with people," said Dez. "They were called pets. People played with them. People even had dogs in their homes. I think dogs live in zoos now."

Dez looked at the dog. The dog put its head up. Dez put his head down. The dog licked Dez. It licked Dez on the chin.

"What is it doing?" asked Jax. "Is it trying to eat you?"

"No," said Dez. "It is licking me. Dogs like to lick. Dogs lick when they like you."

Dez patted the dog. He rubbed it on the head. The dog's tail began to wag.

HEY, LITTLE GUY

"What is it doing now?" asked Jax. "Is it shaking?"

"No," said Dez. "It is wagging its tail.

That means it is happy."

Jax looked at the dog. He did not put out his hand. He did not pat the dog.

"Why is the dog in the bike pack?" asked Jax.

"I don't know," said Dez. "It is very odd. We must take it back to the little girl. We must ask her about the dog. She can tell us. She can tell us why the dog is in her pack."

Dez closed the pack. He held it in one arm. Then the boys flew down the sky path. The boys flew to school.

9
THE DOG

Soon Dez and Jax got to school. They saw Mr. Munn. They saw the little girl. She was with her mom. The girl and her mom were waiting. They were waiting for the boys. Dez and Jax flew up to the girl.

"You have my pack!" she said. "Thank you!" The little girl went to Dez. She grabbed the pack.

"Thank you," said her mom. "Thank you for finding Lissy's pack."

Dez was glad. He liked to make kids happy.

"We are glad you got the pack," said Mr. Munn. "Lissy told me you would be late."

Dez and Jax needed to go into school. But Dez had to know about the dog.

"We are glad to help," said Dez. "We like to help kids. But tell me. Tell me why Lissy has a dog. Why was a dog in her pack?"

LISSY HAS SOME EXPLAINING TO DO!

Lissy opened her pack. She patted the

dog. The dog licked Lissy. The dog wagged its tail.

"The dog is mine," said Lissy's mom. "The dog is from my work. I have a job at a lab. We take care of dogs. We help dogs grow. We help dogs to like people. Dogs and people used to be friends. We want dogs and people to be friends again."

DOG GROWTH POTION

"That is good," said Dez. "But why does Lissy have the dog?" He patted the dog. Jax watched.

"Lissy should not have the dog," said her

mom. She frowned at Lissy. "She took the dog. I did not see her take it. She put it in her pack."

"I wanted to take the dog to school," said Lissy. "I wanted to show my friends."

"It is not safe for the dog to go to school," said Lissy's mom. "Some kids do not like dogs. The dog will be sad. The dog may get hurt. The dog must go home. I am taking the dog home with me. You must go to school now."

Lissy looked sad. She patted the dog one more time. Then she left. She went into the school.

"Good-bye," said Dez. "We have to go to school too."

"Good-bye," said Lissy's mom. "Thank you for saving the dog."

Dez patted the dog one more time. Jax watched. Then Dez and Jax went into school with Mr. Munn.

10
THE WINNER

It was Friday. Friday was school meeting day. At the end of the day, all the kids went to the meeting. Lots of kids talked at the meeting. Lots of teachers talked at the meeting. Mr. Munn talked too. He talked about the contest.

"Now it is contest time," said Mr. Munn. "It is time to see which Sky Watcher had the most spinner shots. Who will be the winner this week?"

Jax and Dez were sitting with the other Sky Watchers. They were waiting. They were all waiting to hear the winner.

"There were lots of good shots this week," said Mr. Munn. "The Sky Watchers are doing a good job."

TO THE
SKY WATCHERS

Jax looked at Dez. "You did a great job. You had eight shots. I hope you are the winner."

"We'll see," said Dez. He hoped he was

the winner too.

Mr. Munn looked at all the Sky Watchers. The Sky Watchers looked at Mr. Munn.

"The winner this week is Kath!" said Mr. Munn. "Kath had nine spinner shots."

Kath jumped up. She had a big grin. She went to Mr. Munn. He gave her a ticket. The ticket gave her free time at the game center.

KATH JUMPING FOR JOY

"Nine is better than eight," said Dez. "Kath beat me. Kath did a great job."

"I'm sorry," said Jax. "I'm sorry that you didn't win." Jax looked pretty sad.

"It's okay," said Dez. "We will keep

shooting spinners. We will both try to win next week."

"Yes, but you should have won," said Jax. "You should have shot that last spinner. Not me. Then you would have nine shots. Then you and Kath would both win."

"That's okay," said Dez. "I'm glad I grabbed Lissy's pack. I'm glad I saved the dog."

Dez and Jax got up. It was time to go home. It was time for the Sky Watchers to watch. They had to watch the sky path while the other kids went home.

"Look," said Jax. "There's Lissy's mom."

Dez saw Lissy's mom. She was at the door. She was looking for someone. Dez went up to her.

"Hi," said Dez.

"There you are," said Lissy's mom. "I was looking for you."

"Me? Why?" asked Dez.

"I have a big question," she said. She looked at a pack on the floor near her feet. "I have a big question for you."

Dez wondered what the question could be. Why would Lissy's mom have a question for him?

"I went to work," said Lissy's mom. "I told my workers about you. I told them how you saved the dog. They were very glad. They said you were very brave."

Dez grinned. "It was fun," he said. "It was

fun to save the pack. It was fun to find the dog. I really liked the dog."

Lissy's mom nodded. "Yes," she said. "The dog liked you too. At my job we are looking for people who like dogs. We need to find them. We need them to do some work for us."

Dez frowned. "What kind of work?" he asked.

"We need people to care for the dogs," she said. "We need people to hold the dogs and pat the dogs. We want the dogs to like people. We want the dogs to become pets again." Lissy's mom bent down. She opened the pack on the floor. There was the dog. Lissy's mom lifted up the dog. She held the dog out to Dez.

Dez took the dog. The dog looked up at Dez. It licked him on the chin. Dez patted the dog. The dog wagged its tail.

SLOBBERY MESS

"Are you asking me to keep this dog?" asked Dez. "Are you asking me to care for this dog?"

"Yes," said Lissy's mom. "We would like you to keep the dog as a pet. I called your mom. She said yes. But I need you to say yes."

Dez rubbed the dog some more. The dog wagged its tail harder. Dez looked at Lissy's mom.

"Yes," said Dez. "I will keep the dog. It will be my pet." Then Dez looked at Jax. "It looks like I'm a winner after all," said Dez with a big grin.